Lee Aucoin, *Creative Director*
Jamey Acosta, *Senior Editor*
Heidi Fiedler, *Editor*
Produced and designed by
Denise Ryan & Associates
Illustration © Jack Hughes
Rachelle Cracchiolo, *Publisher*

Teacher Created Materials

5301 Oceanus Drive
Huntington Beach, CA 92649-1030
http://www.tcmpub.com
Paperback: ISBN: 978-1-4333-5455-7
Library Binding: ISBN: 978-1-4807-1134-1
© 2014 Teacher Created Materials

D1540634

Edward the Explorer

Written by James Reid
Illustrated by Jack Hughes

I am Edward the Explorer.
I am brave and bold.

Every day, I look near and far.

Then, I draw what I see in my notebook.

Monday

I climb over big mountains.

Tuesday

I dive in deep seas.

Wednesday

I row down long rivers.

Thursday

I climb up tall trees.

Friday
I fly over wide canyons.

An explorer—that's me!